First published by Parragon in 2012

Parragon
Queen Street House
4 Queen Street
Bath BA1 1HE, UK
www.parragon.com

ISBN 978-1-4454-9328-2

Printed in China

Sleep Tight, Sleepy Bears

PaRRagon

Bath • New York • Singapore • Hong Kong • Cologne • Delhi
Melbourne • Amsterdam • Johannesburg • Shenzhen

There was a **big** sleepy bear,

and a little sleepy bear.

The big sleepy bear yawned

a great big yawn,

and the little sleepy
bear yawned
a little sleepy yawn.

Then the great
big bear

gave a great big
s t r e t c h ,

and the little sleepy bear gave a little sleepy
s t r e t c h .

Then the **big** sleepy bear got into bed,

and the little sleepy bear got into bed.

Then the **big** sleepy bear put his head on the pillow,

and the little sleepy bear
put his head on the pillow.

Then the **big** sleepy bear
closed his eyes,

and the little sleepy bear closed his eyes.

Then the big sleepy bear sang

a sleepy song:

When I lay me down

to sleep

Four bright angels

around me keep.

Two to watch me through the night.

And two to wake me come daylight.

And the little sleepy bear sang

a sleepy song:

When I lay me down

to sleep

Four bright angels

around me keep.

Two to watch me through the night.

And two to wake me come daylight.

Softer
and
softer
and
softer.

Then the **big** sleepy bear

closed his eyes,

and the little

sleepy bear

closed his eyes.

And the little sleepy bear
thought of the darkness,
and the starlight,

and the big round moon,

and how he'd be sleeping soon.

Then the **big** sleepy
bear whispered,
"Sleep tight."

And the little sleepy bear didn't say a word because he was sound asleep.